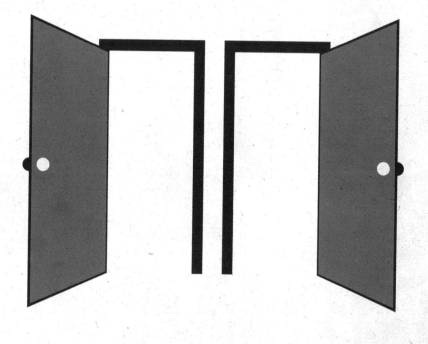

BuyMeToys.Com Presents

THE WOZNDERLAND CHRONICLES ™

PRELUDE

THE OZ/WONDERLAND CHRONICLES
CREATED BY:
BEN AVERY & CASEY HEYING

SCRIPT BY:
BEN AVERY

ILLUSTRATED BY:
CASEY HEYING
TEDDY RIAWAN
BRIANNA GARCIA
PEDRO MAIA

COLORS BY:
CASEY HEYING, OMI REMALANTE JR.
ANDREW HIBNER & MICHAEL BIRKHOFER

LETTERS BY:

OZ/WONDERLAND KIDS
BY
BEN AVERY
ALAN SCHELL
YINA GOH

All Licensing Inquires Should be Directed To Casey Heying at BuyMeToys.Com (574) 271-8697

ISBN: 978-0-9828750-2-5

BuyMeToys.Com Presents

THE W**OZ**NDERLAND CHRONICLES ™

Prelude

THE WONDERLAND CHRONICLES

What you hold in your hands is, technically, the first The Oz/Wonderland Chronicles story . . . if you like to read things in chronological order. But it was written after Book One and Book Two and, in my opinion, should be read after you have read those other two The Oz/Wonderland Chronicles books.

Don't worry. If you read this first, nothing will be spoiled for you. I only suggest reading it this way because that's the order I experienced the story in myself, as I scripted it.

(And I'm the sort of guy who always reads The Lion, the Witch, and the Wardrobe first and The Magician's Nephew sixth, even though The Magician's Nephew takes place first. Do not believe the publisher: The Lion, the Witch, and the Wardrobe may have the number "2" on the spine, but it is book one!)

That said, if you haven't read the other two books, don't worry about this book being just a prequel. Like most prequels, characters in this book come from the other two books -- most notably Alice and Dorothy -- and events in this book explain why some things happened in the other books. That's one reason to have a prequel.

But it's not the only reason we created this book. Like book one and book two, this book is a stand-alone story. The story of a girl: Sarah.

Most characters in this series come from existing fantasy worlds in the public domain, or are inspired by archetypes. My hope has always been that when you see a character, you either know exactly who they are (like Alice and Dorothy) or you at least know the type (like the three Norns who come from Norse mythology). If I've done my job correctly, anyway.

So when you meet Mr. Raven in this book, you don't need to have read George MacDonald's book Lilith. It's a good book, and if you like fantasy literature I recommend reading it at least once, if only to see where C.S. Lewis and J.R.R. Tolkien were getting their inspiration from. But if I've done my job, you don't need to have read it. Mr. Raven shows up, does his thing, and his thing should speak for itself.

Sarah is another story, though. She is a new character. No actual, concrete, literary precedence. This is on purpose. For this book, we needed someone new, who is walking through these worlds fresh. Yes, we are placing her on the board to set up the pieces for the grand finale. And yes, with this book all the pieces are now in place for the last chapter in the Chronicles (at least as far as the story started in book one is concerned). And yes, as said before, this book is a prequel, so it fleshes out some of the backstory only alluded to in previous books. And yes, Sarah plays a very important role in the aforementioned grand finale.

But for now, and most importantly, this is Sarah's story. Her story includes some of our old friends. Her story affects some of our old friends. Her story is affected by some of our old friends. But this is her story. And her story is a story I've wanted to tell for a long time.

And, now that it is in your hands, gentle reader, her story is also your story, to experience and hopefully enjoy.

~ Ben Avery

Star Crossed Lovers

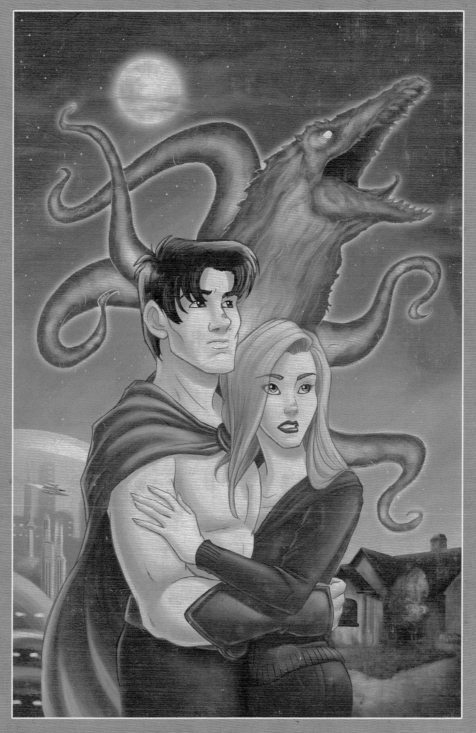

By Mae Mannering

THE WOZNDERLAND CHRONICLES ™

PRELUDE
CHAPTER ONE

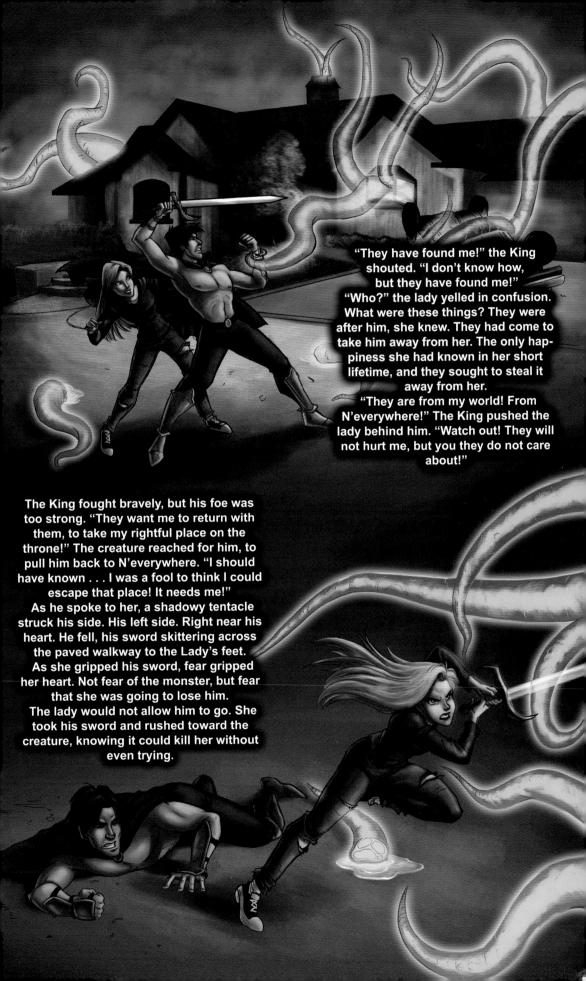

"They have found me!" the King shouted. "I don't know how, but they have found me!"

"Who?" the lady yelled in confusion. What were these things? They were after him, she knew. They had come to take him away from her. The only happiness she had known in her short lifetime, and they sought to steal it away from her.

"They are from my world! From N'everywhere!" The King pushed the lady behind him. "Watch out! They will not hurt me, but you they do not care about!"

The King fought bravely, but his foe was too strong. "They want me to return with them, to take my rightful place on the throne!" The creature reached for him, to pull him back to N'everywhere. "I should have known . . . I was a fool to think I could escape that place! It needs me!"

As he spoke to her, a shadowy tentacle struck his side. His left side. Right near his heart. He fell, his sword skittering across the paved walkway to the Lady's feet.

As she gripped his sword, fear gripped her heart. Not fear of the monster, but fear that she was going to lose him.

The lady would not allow him to go. She took his sword and rushed toward the creature, knowing it could kill her without even trying.

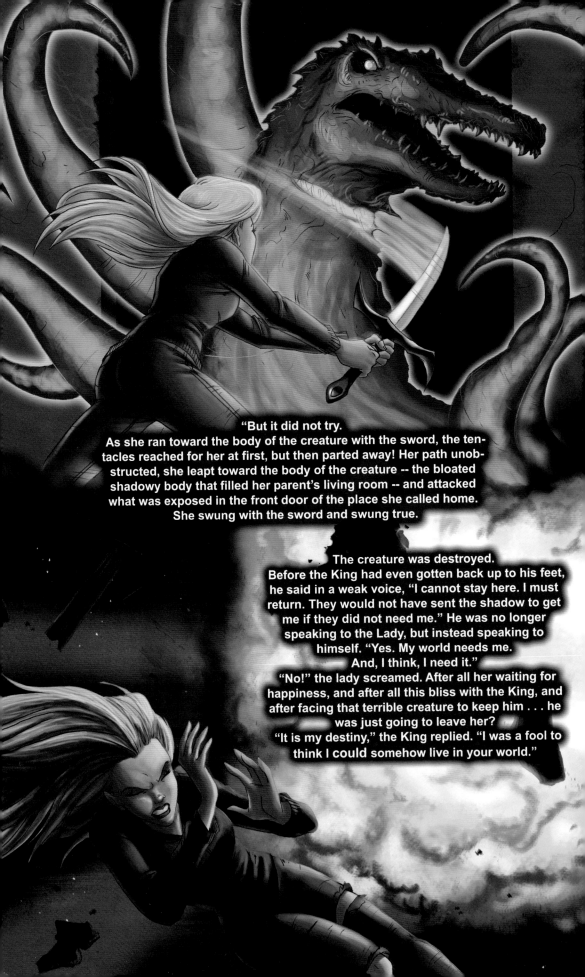

"But it did not try.
As she ran toward the body of the creature with the sword, the tentacles reached for her at first, but then parted away! Her path unobstructed, she leapt toward the body of the creature -- the bloated shadowy body that filled her parent's living room -- and attacked what was exposed in the front door of the place she called home. She swung with the sword and swung true.

The creature was destroyed.
Before the King had even gotten back up to his feet, he said in a weak voice, "I cannot stay here. I must return. They would not have sent the shadow to get me if they did not need me." He was no longer speaking to the Lady, but instead speaking to himself. "Yes. My world needs me. And, I think, I need it."
"No!" the lady screamed. After all her waiting for happiness, and after all this bliss with the King, and after facing that terrible creature to keep him . . . he was just going to leave her?
"It is my destiny," the King replied. "I was a fool to think I could somehow live in your world."

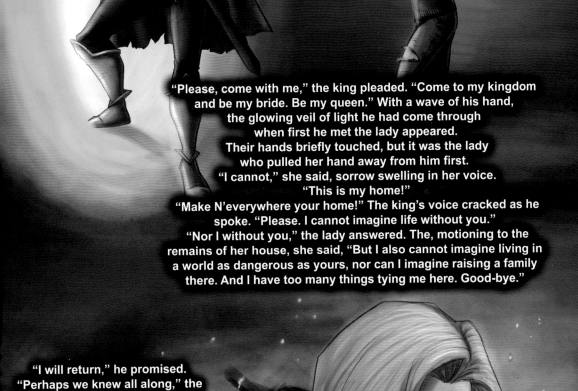

"Please, come with me," the king pleaded. "Come to my kingdom and be my bride. Be my queen." With a wave of his hand, the glowing veil of light he had come through when first he met the lady appeared.
Their hands briefly touched, but it was the lady who pulled her hand away from him first.
"I cannot," she said, sorrow swelling in her voice. "This is my home!"
"Make N'everywhere your home!" The king's voice cracked as he spoke. "Please. I cannot imagine life without you."
"Nor I without you," the lady answered. The, motioning to the remains of her house, she said, "But I also cannot imagine living in a world as dangerous as yours, nor can I imagine raising a family there. And I have too many things tying me here. Good-bye."

"I will return," he promised.
"Perhaps we knew all along," the King said, "this was not meant to be. Our love was doomed from the moment we laid eyes on each other."
"Doomed?" the lady whispered.
"Perhaps." But he did not hear. The King of N'everywhere stepped through and was gone.
The lady did not cry, but not one day passed after that she didn't wonder what would have happened if she had tried to make his world her home.

YOU'RE NOT A REPORTER, ARE YOU?

WHY DO YOU SAY THAT?

FIRST OF ALL, NO ONE CARES ABOUT THIS BOOK EXCEPT MY DIE-HARD FANS WHO WANT TO READ EVERYTHING I'VE WRITTEN.

SECOND OF ALL, YOU'RE LOOKING AT IT RIGHT NOW LIKE YOU'VE NEVER SEEN IT BEFORE, AND IF YOU REALLY WANTED TO INTERVIEW ME ABOUT IT YOU'D HAVE DONE YOUR RESEARCH BEFORE YOU CAME.

AND THIRD, NO OFFENSE, BUT...

YOU DON'T REALLY LOOK THE PART.

YOU'RE RIGHT. I'M NOT A REPORTER.

LISTEN, I DON'T MIND TALKING TO PEOPLE ABOUT MY WORK.

I'M QUITE EASY TO CONTACT THROUGH MY WEBSITE, AND I ANSWER ALL E-MAILS THAT COME TO ME.

BUT YOU MISREPRESENTED YOURSELF TO MY AGENT TO GET ME MEET YOU HERE UNDER FALSE PRETENSES.

I DO NOT APPRECIATE THAT.

PLEASE, MS. MANNERING, HEAR ME OUT.

YOU'VE JUST ABOUT USED UP ANY GOODWILL I HAVE LEFT.

IT'S JUST THAT MY EMPLOYER HAS FOUND A CERTAIN RESONANCE WITH YOUR BOOK HERE.

HE WOULD LIKE TO KNOW ABOUT THE CIRCUMSTANCES THAT LED TO YOUR WRITING IT.

THIS WAS MY SECOND BOOK, AFTER *"LOCKED IN THE GARDEN WITH PAN"*.

THEY WERE BOTH PRETTY MUCH JUST A VANITY PROJECT FOR ME. I SELF-PUBLISHED A SMALL PRINT RUN OF A THOUSAND COPIES.

THEY REALLY AREN'T WORTH MUCH EXCEPT AS A NOVELTY FOR MY FINN MCCOOL FANS.

MY EMPLOYER WAS LED TO BELIEVE *"LOCKED IN A GARDEN WITH PAN"* WAS SOMETHING THAT HAD ACTUALLY HAPPENED TO YOU.

YES, WELL, I WAS LOCKED IN KENSINGTON GARDENS ONCE, AS A CHILD.

THE HALF-GOAT/HALF-BOY AND FAIRY STUFF, THOUGH? I HOPE HE DOESN'T THINK THAT'S PART OF THE *"TRUE STORY"*.

AND THIS ONE?

AS FOR THAT ONE, IT SEEMED TO WRITE ITSELF. THE CHARACTERS JUST SORT OF CAME TO ME, AND I RECORDED WHAT THEY DID.

THE CHARACTER OF *"THE LADY"*? SHE WAS NOT BASED ON ANY REAL PERSON?

IF SHE IS, I DON'T KNOW HER.

WHY ARE YOU ASKING ME THIS?

DO YOU INTEND TO WRITE ANY MORE BOOKS LIKE THIS ONE?

BOOKS THAT *"WRITE THEMSELVES"*?

NO. THE MARKET DOESN'T WANT CHILDREN'S BOOKS THAT AREN'T FOR CHILDREN.

I'LL BE WRITING THE ADVENTURES OF FINN MCCOOL FOR THE TIME BEING.

MARKET FORCES ASIDE, YOU HAVE WRITTEN MORE LIKE THIS, HAVEN'T YOU?

PERHAPS EVEN MORE ABOUT THIS LADY?

NO. NOT ABOUT "THE LADY".

THANK YOU SO MUCH FOR YOUR PATIENCE.

I APOLOGIZE FOR THE DECEPTION.

WHAT JUST HAPPENED HERE?

HEY YOU FORGOT YOUR BOOK...

OH, WOULD IT BE POSSIBLE FOR YOU TO SIGN IT FOR ME?

HELLO, SIR.

AND THE BOOK?

FICTION.

YOU'RE SURE?

SHE WAS NOT LYING.

AND WHAT HAPPENED AFTER THE KING LEFT, I WONDER?

VERY WELL. SHE BELIEVES IT TO BE FICTION. WE WILL COME BACK TO HER. BUT FOR NOW SHE SEEMS TO BE A DEAD END.

LET'S MOVE ON. I HAVE NO PRESSING LEADS RIGHT NOW. I WILL CONTACT YOU IF ANYTHING COMES UP.

YES, SIR.

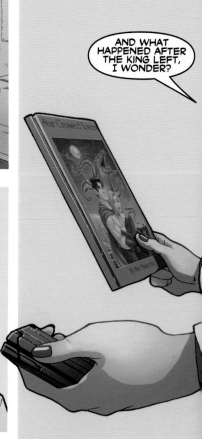

THE W⊘NDERLAND CHRONICLES ™

PRELUDE
CHAPTER TWO

IF YOU HADN'T COME TO COLLEGE IN CHICAGO, YOU'D NEVER HAVE MET ME!

YOU'D HAVE NEVER MET ANY OF YOUR GREAT FRIENDS IF YOU HADN'T LEFT KANSAS!

RIGHT...

JUST REST, MS. HELMS!

EXCUSE ME, I'M SARAH HELMS... IS MY MOTHER IN THERE?

YES. YOU CAN GO RIGHT ON IN. SHE'S IN STABLE CONDITION.

BE PREPARED, THOUGH. SHE WAS ROUGHED UP PRETTY BADLY.

DO YOU KNOW WHAT HAPPENED?

YOUR MOTHER WON'T SAY.

BUT I WOULD SAY YOUR MOTHER SHOULD PROBABLY GET OUT OF HER CURRENT SITUATION.

HAVE YOU SEEN ANY SIGNS OF ABUSE? OTHER THAN WHAT YOU'RE ABOUT TO SEE WHEN YOU OPEN THAT DOOR?

WITH HER CURRENT BOYFRIEND? NOT YET.

BUT IT WAS ONLY A MATTER OF TIME. SHE ATTRACTS THOSE KINDS OF GUYS...

YOU SHOULD ENCOURAGE YOUR MOTHER TO GET HELP.

OH, AND WE NEED YOUR MOTHER'S INSURANCE INFORMATION SO WE CAN PROCESS THE BILLING PAPERWORK.

RIGHT.

ANYONE SITTING THERE?

WHAT?

YOU LOOK LIKE SOMEONE WHO COULD USE COMPANY. AND I COULD USE A LITTLE COMPANY NOW, TOO.

YOUR FRIEND, HER UNCLE OR WHATEVER, IS HE OKAY?

NO. NO...

I DON'T SEE HOW IT'S POSSIBLE TO BE SURROUNDED BY ALL THOSE MEDICAL PROFESSIONALS AND ALL THAT EQUIPMENT AND MEDICINE AND STILL DIE, BUT...

I'M SORRY.

ME TOO.

I DECIDED TO GET OUT OF THE WAY, WHILE THEY TAKE CARE OF BUSINESS UP THERE.

MY NAME'S ALICE.

SARAH.

IT SOUNDED LIKE THERE WAS A BIT OF A COMMOTION IN YOUR ROOM, TOO, BEFORE EVERYTHING HIT THE FAN IN OUR ROOM. ARE YOU OKAY?

NO.

WHAT?

GET YOUR HANDS OFF ME!

WHAT ARE YOU DOING HERE?

THE DOCTORS NEED HER INSURANCE INFORMATION, SO I CAME TO GET IT!

WHAT ARE YOU DOING HERE, ERIC? YOUR GIRLFRIEND IS IN THE HOSPITAL!

YOU SHOULDN'T HAVE COME HERE!

I WOULDN'T HAVE TO IF YOU'D HAVE GONE WITH MOM!

BUT, I GUESS ACCOMPANYING SOMEONE IN THE HOSPITAL ISN'T REALLY SUCH A GREAT IDEA, HUHN?

SARAH, THAT WASN'T ME! IT WAS...I DON'T KNOW WHAT IT WAS...

BUT IT WAS AFTER YOU, SARAH! I HEARD IT SAY YOUR NAME WHEN IT ATTACKED YOUR MOTHER!

IT HURT YOUR MOTHER BECAUSE IT WAS LOOKING FOR YOU!

I CAME HERE BECAUSE I WAS AFRAID THAT YOU'D COME HOME AND IT WOULD COME HERE AFTER YOU!

BAM BAM

CLICK
CLICK

SAAAARAAAAAH

NO!

SARAH!

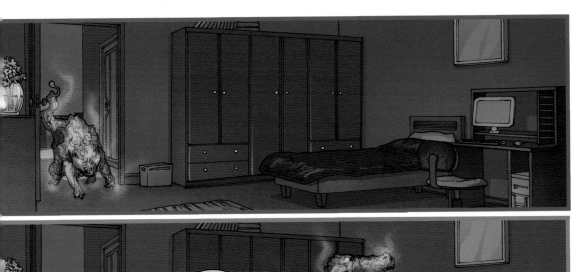

THE WOZNDERLAND CHRONICLES ™

PRELUDE
CHAPTER THREE

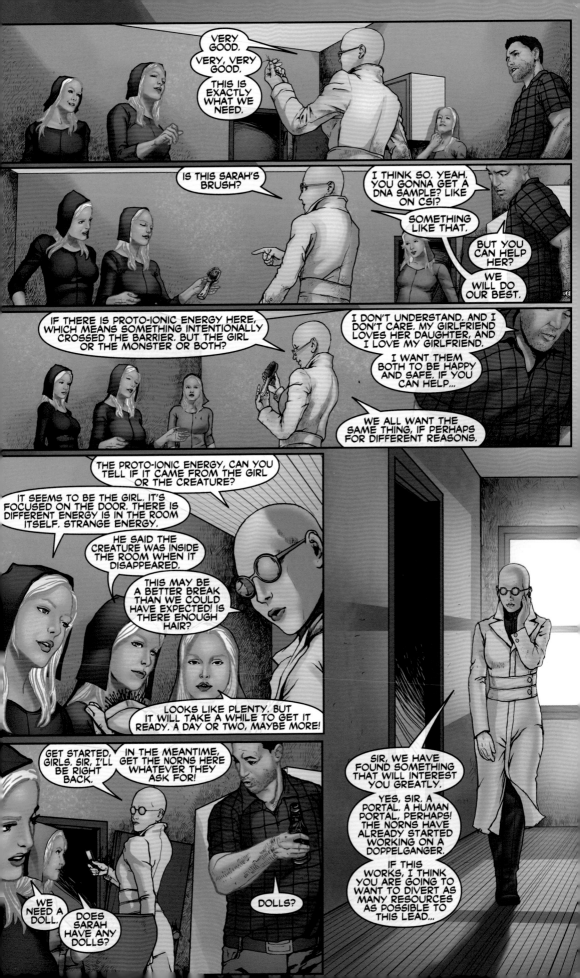

OZ, EARLY THE NEXT MORNING.

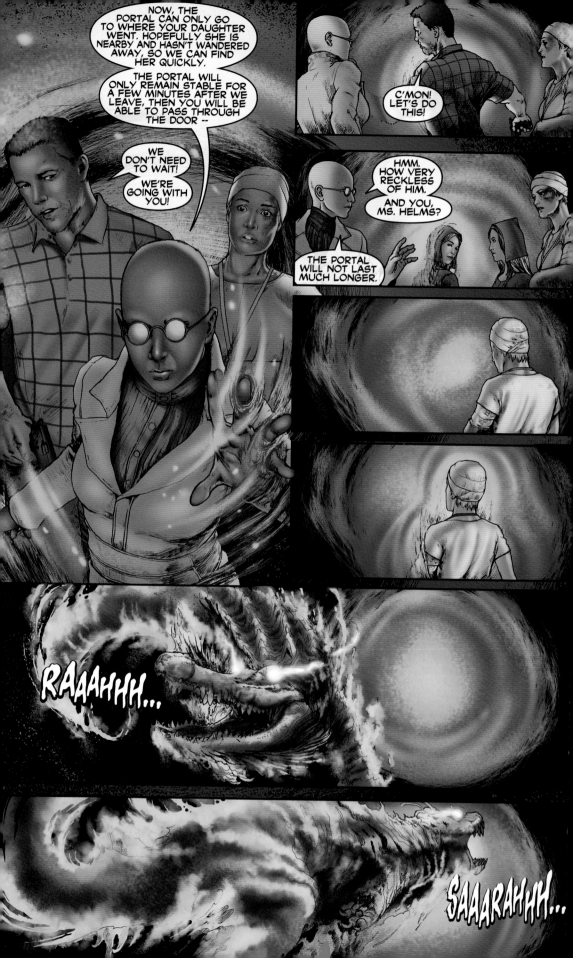

THE WONDERLAND CHRONICLES ™

PRELUDE
CHAPTER FOUR

I AM READY TO LEAVE THE MOMENT YOU ARE.

WHAT? WHY? THIS IS YOUR DREAM!

FIRST OF ALL, I PROMISED GLINDA I WOULD PROTECT YOU, AND I AM NOTHING IF NOT A FROG OF MY WORD! I WILL STAY BY YOUR SIDE UNTIL YOU ARE SAFE.

FROGMAN, I *AM* SAFE.

SECONDLY, THOSE LADY FROGS WERE A BIT BENEATH MY STATION, DON'T YOU THINK?

"BENEATH YOUR STATION"!?! FROGMAN, I THOUGHT THIS IS WHAT YOU SAID YOU WERE LONGING FOR ALL YOUR LIFE!

"ALL MY LIFE" WAS A BIT OF AN EXAGGERATION...

I MEAN, I REALLY DIDN'T DESIRE IT UNTIL THE DEMISE OF ALL THE SKOSH PLANTS, WHEN I REALIZED NO OTHER FROG PEOPLE LIKE ME COULD COME INTO BEING. "DON'T KNOW WHAT YOU WANT UNTIL IT'S GONE" AND ALL THAT ROT...

BUT I WAS TAKEN UP IN THE MUSIC AND THE MOMENT LAST NIGHT. YES, IT SEEMED LIKE WHAT I WAS LOOKING FOR. BUT IN TRUTH, I'M NOT JUST LOOKING FOR A FEMALE HUMAN-SIZED FROG...

YOU'RE LOOKING FOR A FEMALE YOU.

PRECISELY.

UNBELIEVABLE.

NO, I BELIEVE IT TO BE QUITE BELIEVABLE.

WELL, I, FOR ONE, HAVE NO INTENTION OF LEAVING ANY TIME SOON.

THERE'S NO WITCHES, NO MONSTERS, AND NO BOYFRIENDS -- MINE OR MY MOTHER'S -- AND I LIKE IT JUST FINE!

I SUGGEST YOU GET OVER YOUR PREJUDICES AND JUST ENJOY THE COMPANY OF THOSE HOTTIE FROGS WHO, IN CASE YOU HADN'T NOTICED, SEEM TO LIKE YOU!

THEY HAVE, INDEED, TAKEN A SHINE TO ME.

FROM WHAT WE UNDERSTAND, SHE ARRIVED WITH A FRIEND, A MAN-CROW TYPE OF CREATURE.

NO ACCOUNTING FOR TASTE.

FOLLOW ME!

THEY WERE ATTACKED BY A WICKED WITCH, BUT FORTUNATELY GLINDA, THE GOOD WITCH, WAS NEARBY.

THE GIRL AND THE RAVEN MAN, ALONG WITH A FRIEND OF OURS, MR. FROGMAN, ESCAPED TO SAFETY WHILE GLINDA FOUGHT THE WICKED WITCH.

WHEN THE WITCH DISAPPEARED, GLINDA WAS ABLE TO CHECK ON THE GIRL AND THE BIRD MAN AND FROGMAN, THERE WAS NO TRACE OF THEM.

ANOTHER PORTAL?

PERHAPS... I SENSE NO ENERGY YET...

KEEP THE PROVERBIAL EYE OPEN.

ALWAYS.

ANYWAY, YOU'LL EXCUSE US IF WE'RE ALL A BIT JUMPY.

THERE HASN'T BEEN A WICKED WITCH IN OZ FOR A LONG TIME.

...WE'RE ALL A BIT WORRIED ABOUT WHAT THIS MEANS FOR US.

DIDJA HEAR THAT?

HEAR WHAT? I DIDN'T HEAR ANYTHING.

WHAT'S WRONG?

NOTHING, DON'T MIND LION.

HE'S AFRAID OF HIS OWN SHADOW.

THIS IS WHERE THEY DISAPPEARED.

GLINDA SENT THEM TO HIDE IN THE TUNNELS BENEATH THE HILLS, BUT THE WITCH CAVED IT IN BEFORE THEY EVEN GOT INSIDE.

BUT THEY WENT THROUGH ANYWAY, AND WERE GONE.

SHE MUST HAVE OPENED A NEW PORTAL.

BUT WHERE TO?

WE'LL KNOW SOON ENOUGH.

THIS ONE'S FRESHER THAN THE LAST ONE, IT'LL BE EVEN EASIER TO OPEN.

HM?

SARAH... WHERE ARE YOU GOING?

DO YOU KNOW?

TIN MAN?

WHAT?

EVE, DID SHE GO THROUGH HERE?

YES.

WHERE DOES IT GO?

OUR WORLD, SOMEWHERE, I WOULD ASSUME.

THE THING ABOUT BEING AFRAID OF YOUR OWN SHADOW IS...

RWAAARRR!

RWAAAAHHH

UHN.

NO!

IT'S GOING AFTER SARAH!

IT WAS ATTACKING YOU LIKE IT HAD SOME SORT OF GRUDGE!

IT JUST MIGHT!

WE HAVE TO SAVE SARAH!

LATER...

LOOK AT YOU! YOUR DREAM HAS COME TRUE!

AND SOON, WILL WE HEAR THE PITTER PATTER OF LITTLE TADPOLES AROUND HERE?

WE'RE NOT SURE IF THAT ASPECT OF THINGS WILL WORK...

FIRST WE NEEDS TA BE COURTIN'!

IT DOESN'T MATTER, THOUGH, DOES IT FROGMAN? YOU'RE NO LONGER ALONE. AND ME?

I'M NOT JUST A QUEEN, I'M A GOD! THIS WORLD NEEDED LIFE, AND I HAVE BROUGHT IT!

I'M IN ABSOLUTE CONTROL FOR THE FIRST TIME!

WAIT, I JUST REALIZED ONE MORE THING TO MAKE THIS JUST PERFECT...I WONDER IF SHE'S DONE WITH IT YET...

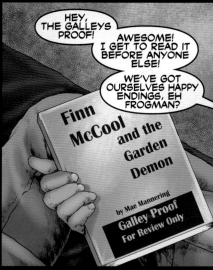

HEY, THE GALLEYS PROOF!

AWESOME! I GET TO READ IT BEFORE ANYONE ELSE!

WE'VE GOT OURSELVES HAPPY ENDINGS, EH FROGMAN?

Finn McCool and the Garden Demon

by Mae Mannering

Galley Proof
For Review Only

THE MIDDLE REALM. "EARTH."

THAT ONE... HURT...

BODY #8, I'LL BE SEEING YOU SOON, THE MAJOR IS GOING TO KILL *THIS* BODY AFTER I MAKE MY REPORT...

THE BEGINNING

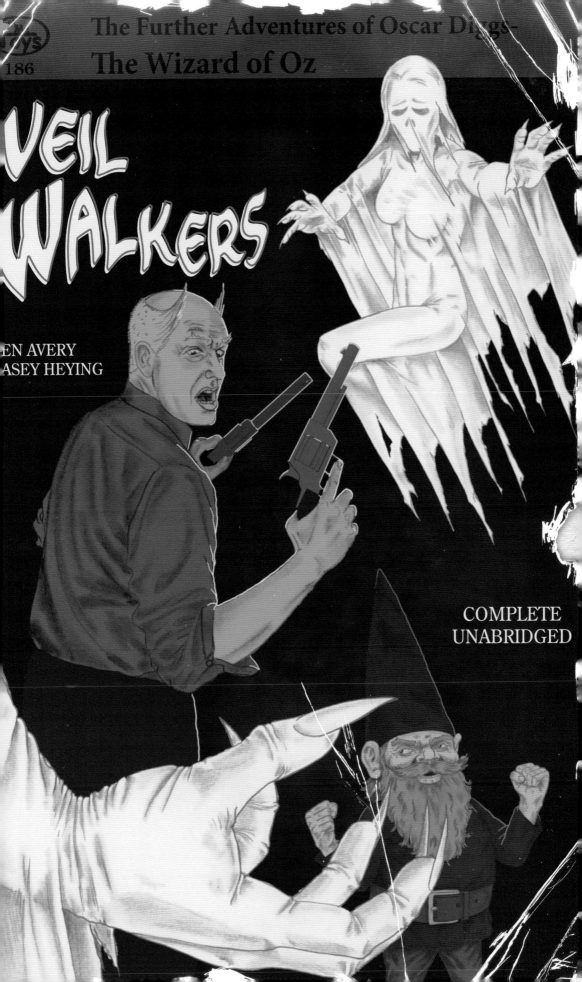

The Further Adventures of Oscar Diggs-
The Wizard of Oz

VEIL WALKERS

A Novel By
Ben Avery & Casey Heying

Illustrations By
Casey Heying

Complete and Unabridged

Published with Special Arrangement with
BuyMeToys.Com

Chapter 1
In Which Wars Are Fought, Amours Are Spurned, and Doors Are Closed

"This is your fault, you know," Oz shouted as loud as possible to the copilot in the seat beside him. The engine of the photonic powered bi-plane roared as he pulled back on the stick, pushing the plane into a vertical climb and narrowly avoiding an explosion.

"I know, I know," Roland, the gnome replied, shouting just as loud. "I have no hope! Womans, they love me. My greatest strength! And I love womans. My greatest weakness!" Wistfully, no longer yelling, he said, "I have blessings . . . I have curses . . ."

Oz frowned and spun the plane back around, diving back toward the action. "I had almost finished it! I was ready to test it! And then you go and start a war!"

"Where are you going?" Roland screamed. Other photonic bi-planes darted around them, firing their light cannons at the enemy: the army of the Amazonian queen, Queen Titania. The three dozen women ranged in size from forty to fifty feet tall. Clad in armor and bearing spears, swords, and bows and arrows, they might have been at a disadvantage against the scores of photonic biplanes with their light cannons and missiles. They might have, if the light cannons were able to pierce the armor or the missiles were able to deliver an explosion that was more than a bee sting, relatively speaking.

The Amazonians were at a disadvantage as well, of course. The air force of the Cloud Queen had its numbers, and beyond that they were maneuverable and quick. The Amazonian's weapons, if they struck true, would destroy the biplanes of the Cloud Clingers. But it was striking true that was the difficulty.

It made for a mismatched war, and one that had few casualties, mainly because there had been little time for developing new, more effective weapons. Oz knew that process had already started, at least on the Clouds. He was certain it had started in the Amazonian nation as well. Until now, the Amazonians and Cloud Clingers had never needed to go to war. They shared and traded resources and knowledge, and in the one war this world had known before this one -- an invasion of telepathic space locusts -- the two nations were staunch allies.

But Roland had managed to change all that. Generations of peace and friendship gone because of a two-foot six inch tall gnome. "Forty-two dimensions, three alternate realities, two distant galaxies, four trips into the past, and two into the future . . . and somehow, wherever we go, you manage to anger the one female who should not be angered in all of them!"

"Two!" Roland corrected.

"What?"

"Well," Roland said, with a voice that managed to sound both shamed and proud at the same time, "both Queen Titania and Queen Avion have fallen in love with me! So technically speaking, I've angered both of them! Queen Avion because I cheated on her, and Queen Titania because I told her I planned to stay with Queen Avion!"

Oz shook his head, jerking the plane to the side and narrowly missing an arrow. The Amazonians had changed their tactics and were no longer targeting individuals. They were now just firing randomly into the cloud of biplanes.

"I had almost figured out how to use the photonic energy to open a portal to get us out of here!" Oz's chest was heavy with anger. That wasn't good. He need to be alert and panicky. He always thought better when he had the adrenaline boost a good panic gave him. Anger made his thought processes sluggish. "If I had been able to figure out how to do that we would have a machine that would take us from realm to realm at will! We'd be in control of the journey home instead of finding random portals that took us wherever they happened to lead!"

"What can be said by me?" Roland sighed. "I have sorrow! I do! But I also have love . . . for two lovers! Ah, my life has so many complications!"

The enormous hand of an Amazonian warrior appeared directly in front of them and Oz dove under it. "I should have never come back for you! I should have left you in Titania's dungeon! I should have just left without you!"

"I have gratefulness that you did not," Roland answered. "That dungeon, it smelled of giant armpits. Them few males the Amazonians keep, they need to shower more."

"Shut up, Roland! I'm trying to think!"

Oz knew two things: first, the only way the war was going to stop was if neither side could have Roland; second, only two things could take Roland away. Death . . . or Oz. And beyond that, the luxury Oz had enjoyed over the past year of free reign in both the Cloud labs and the Amazonian's mines to study the photonic energy source was gone. After what Roland had done, neither of them would trust Oz.

Oz still did not understand the source of the photonic energy. He knew it had something to do with the sun and collecting its rays, but he had never seen energy collection like the Cloud Clingers had perfected. It transformed the energy into something else. Something that could, with the right catalyst, open a portal to another world. And he knew what that catalyst was: the natural Cavorite the Amazonian's mined. In all of Oz's travels, he had never come across naturally occuring Cavorite. Of course, the Amazonians and the Cloud Clingers did not call it Cavorite -- how would they even know of Cavor, the earth man who developed the lighter than air material? They called it "airanium," but Oz knew Cavorite when he saw it. But it was so unstable in this unrefined form, and it created such an explosion when activated by the photonic light beam, that Oz believed it opened the fabric of the universe.

Enough Cavorite and a strong enough beam of photonic energy could create a portal. And if Oz used his magic, perhaps he could even guide the other end of the portal and return, dare he think it . . . home? But that theory was something to test in a lab, not in the middle of a war.

Peace could only come if Oz opened a portal and took that little lothario Roland with him to another world. A world where he would find another woman and . . .

No. He'd worry about the women of that other world later. For now, he had a plan. A plan that might not work at all. A plan that might mean using what little magic from the Land of Oz that he had left. A plan that he would never try if he were actually thinking, but because he was panicking and not thinking straight, a plan that he knew was their only hope.

Spinning the plane sideways to dive between the knees of an Amazonian warrior and then straightening out again and wrenching the stick to the side to narrowly avoid a Cloud Clingers' missile, Oz guided the plane away from the war zone.

"Roland, listen carefully! I want you to get on the wireless and send a message to both Queen Avion and Queen Titania! I want you to say exactly what I am about to tell you to say!" Oz gave Roland his "lines" and then he stood up in the plane and climbed up onto the body of the plane. "Also," he said, "take control of the plane!"

Roland took the controls and tried to hold it steady -- no easy feat for a man half the height of the men who were meant to fly these planes. "What are you doing?"

"I'm going to adjust the light cannons! I have a plan! Just go straight ahead! Aim for the foot of that mountain!" Beneath that mountain was the largest deposit of unrefined Cavorite the Amazonians had yet discovered. Oz edged himself forward, toward the spinning propeller made of solid light. All he had to do was tie in the cannon to the engines.

He opened the engine hatch and wrenched it from its hinges. He let it go, watching it as it tumbled in the plane's slipstream behind them. That was not the only thing behind them. Both the Amazonian army and the Cloud Air Force were following them, fighting each other as they did, Queen Titania and Queen Avion leading their respective troops as they did. The giants' great, powerful strides allowed them to keep pace with the quick little planes. Both groups were even with each other as they chased Oz and Roland, and both groups were catching up.

"Roland! The message!" Oz crept back along the plane and to the wings where the light cannons were mounted. He crawled out on the left wing, pulling at the power tube that delivered the energy for the weapon. The cannon's power came from their own source, a source far less powerful than the engine. He hoped the cannon would even be able to handle the power.

"Ladies," Oz could hear Roland say through the wireless reciever in his helmet. He cringed. Roland already went off script! Oz told him to say "your majesties"! "Ladies, a moment of your time!"

"What is it, my love?" Queen Titania's voice almost seemed to quiver with sadness and loss, even as Oz saw her, out of the corner of his eye, swing her sword brutally at a Cloud Clingers' plane and cutting it in half. "Why has that horrible Professor Oz taken you from me?"

"From you," Queen Avion's angry trill of a voice shouted. "I was the one Roland was to marry!"

Oz crawled back to the engine of the plane, pulling the energy tube as he did. He pulled one of the engine's main lines with a quick tug and almost fell off the plane.

"Sadly, I must tell you," Roland said, his voice twinged with genuine sorrow, "my heart beats with love for both of you! Queen Titania, for your passion! Queen Avion, for your tenderness!"

Oz held the engine mainline and the cannon's power line. They would not connect for a long term energy transfer, but this was strictly a short term proposal.

Especially if it didn't work.

"And the two of you, your majesties," good, Oz thought, he's finally getting something right, "must not blame each other! Direct your hatred to me!"

The plane lurched as the engine tried to take in the photonic energy it needed but could no longer get because Oz had disconnected it.

"Uh, Ozzy, flying, it gets more difficult!" Roland shouted.

"Just keep us going straight and give them the message!"

Oz crawled back onto the wing. He was going to have to fire the cannon manually, now that he had bypassed the original energy source.

"What has Oz done?" Titania roared. She liked Oz enough when he introduced the wireless technology to the Amazonians. Not so much when he started a men's liberation movement among the male underclass.

"It was Oz who took you to the Amazonians in the first place!"

"Don't let them talk," Oz ordered Roland as he inched his way along the wing, holding the top wing with a white knuckled grip and carefully stepping along the bottom wing. "Just tell them what I told you to! We're not just trying to escape, we're trying to stop a war from escalating!"

"Right," Roland said. "So the decision, it carries difficulty," Roland continued. "But with only one me, and that one me, he loves both you womans, no happiness exists in our future! So long as both womans want me, neither woman can have me!"

Oz reached down from the wing to the cannon. "Roland! Aim directly for the mountain!" With one hand, he steadied himself, holding on to the front of the wing. With the other hand, he held the triggering mechanism. "As soon as I fire, get out here on the wing with me! And bring the parachute!

The plane lurched forward and suddenly slowed down. "It doesn't have enough power to get us to the mine!" Roland screeched.

"Stop screaming and finish the message to the queens!" Oz felt the triggering mechanism. He didn't want to shoot too soon or too late.

"Your majesties, good-bye, I bid you," Roland said, "and please, know peace after I leave you!"

Oz pulled the trigger. A blast of uncontrolled photonic energy erupted from the cannon, blasting into the mountain and drilling a hole into the earth. Oz looked back for a brief moment. Queen Titania was right behind them, close enough to reach out her hand . . .

"Now, Roland! The parachute!"

Roland was struggling with the seat, which was also the parachute. "I'm trying! It's bigger than me!"

The heat of the energy burned all of Oz's exposed skin, especially the hand holding the cannon's trigger. He let go of the wing and stretched out his hand, focusing some of the last remnants of the Oz magic he had. The magic would protect them, open a tunnel through the explosion and channel the energy unleashed by the Cavorite/photonic explosion to activate the portal.

Ahead of them, the yellowish bloom of an explosion rushed toward them. But there, in the ground where the energy had blasted a hole, Oz could see the familiar blue glow of an inter-universal portal.

"Roland! Now!"

And then Roland was at his side. Oz slipped the parachute strap over one arm, let go of the cannon with the other arm, grabbed Roland with both hands and jumped forward.

Queen Titania's giant hand snagged the tail section of the plane but it was too late. Oz and Roland were in free fall . . . heading into the explosion.

"No, my love, don't you'll die!" Queen Avion's voice sang in through the wireless earpiece.

Oz smiled. This would work! The Queens would think they had died in the explosion and blame Oz, not each other. In truth they were going to fall right through the explosion, and assuming that did not kill them, fall right through the portal, and assuming the portal is positioned safely, emerge in a new world . . .

***

Oz and Roland sailed through the between place, falling and yet not moving, speeding through space and yet stationary in nothingness.

Was that a face Oz saw?

Was that Roland's voice Oz heard?

No, a chorus of voices.

No, a chorus of silence.

And Roland's voice was mixed in it somehow.

Again, a face. But no. Not a face. Just a . . . being. An essence.

Oz had never experienced travel through a portal like this before. It had always been instantaneous. Had he done something wrong? Was it the mix of raw materials and magic that had thrown them into a new state of being?

How could this be nothingness if he was experiencing it?

Did physics and philosophy mean anything when . . .

***

As Oz and Roland exited the portal, Oz gladly let the existential philosophical musings disappear with the nothingness they left behind them. The plan worked. They were now in free fall a couple thousand feet above some new world.

"Where?" Roland shouted above the whistling wind screaming in their ears.

"Somewhere with no women, I hope," Oz shouted back.

"Me too," Roland shouted, "sort of!"

"Hold tight!" Oz hugged Roland close to his body and Roland grabbed Oz's shirt with all his might. Oz pulled the ripcord for the parachute and they jerked to a relative stop, now gently falling toward a city that became visible beneath them. The details of the tall buildings, made of metal and glass and reaching up toward the sky with colorful blinking lights all over them, lights that formed moving words and pictures and crawled up and down the buildings. The characters that formed the words: they were English, Oz thought as they fell even closer.

Could it be possible?

"Where?" Roland asked again. "Somewhere known?"

Oz nodded, a lump in his throat. "Yes," he managed to say. "It's . . . home."

It had to be. It looked like New York, but New York as he had never seen it before. This was not home as he left it the last time he was here. Close, but not quite. No matter. "I'm home," Oz said as they fell. "And it's the future!"

Chapter 2
In Which a New Life Is Made, a Ghost Receives Aid, and a Universe is Frayed

Henry was dead.

Oz sat in front of the computer, staring at the obituary result he had gotten after searching for his friend's name.

He felt like a, what was the word? 'Stalker.' And in some ways, perhaps, he was. Originally, he had just done the search out of desperate curiosity. He had been gone, away from Earth, for so long. Extended stays in Oz, and then the adventures after, a few times in places where time did not flow as it did in this world, and then there were the occasions he actually traveled through time, both to the past and the future . . . it all meant that his own timeline was a jumble.

Now, he was in the future. He had to know: what had become of Dorothy? What had become of Henry and Em? Of all the humans he had come to know and love while he was in Oz.

Since then, he had been keeping tabs on his old friends. He never made contact with them. They had new lives, and while the traces of Oz still lingered, he expected most of them would have forgotten Oz. To leave such a place as Oz usually meant leaving it behind forever, especially if you left it when you were young . . . relatively speaking, of course -- how many years had he and even Dorothy and her aunt and uncle spent in Oz, not aging?

And so, even though Dorothy had lived long enough in Oz to be an adult now, when she came back to Earth she was still a child. But now, after returning, she aged normally again. She was a bright young college student in Chicago, living a normal life of pizza and boys and books . . . or whatever a normal life looked like for modern college girls.

Come to think of it, Oz mused, he didn't even know what life for college girls of his own original time looked like.

He was just happy that she was happy.

Well, not happy. Not with this news. Not with Henry's death.

But she was safe. There was another reason he kept tabs on her and the others. As he watched them and looked into their doings, he had realized that someone else was watching them. Or if not watching Dorothy and her family specifically, watching for people like them. He didn't know exactly who was doing it, but it seemed to be something sinister. Oz's sources with the "other world underworld," as he liked to call the network of people and creatures who knew about or came from other worlds, confirmed this. Someone, or, more likely, a group of someones, was looking for information about the other realms. Oz dared not reveal himself to his old friends, not only because he did not want to disrupt their new lives by jogging the memory of their old ones, but because he did not want this shadowy group to come across these people he treasured so much.

For the time being, he had his job, teaching history at a small college in a small town in the middle of nowhere.

The middle of nowhere. That's where he liked to be.

He had an apartment.

He had a car.

He had a music player the size of a pack of cigarettes that held every song he had ever heard and then some -- music from his time and the other times he had emerged from Oz.

Of course, he had no cigarettes. Turns out smoking was bad for you. He knew a couple wizards who would be disappointed about that.

And he had Roland.

That was how he got the job in the first place. One of his contacts, a visitor to our world who had been a street vendor in Chicago since Oz's original timeline, had helped Oz get the identification papers he needed to be able to get a job and pay taxes and have a life. But Roland had gotten Oz the job at this college.

Because the college president was a woman. Roland used his unique talent to get her to fall in love with him . . . or perhaps it was President Underwood who used his unique talent to get him to fall in love with her . . . Oz could never really tell how it worked with Roland. Somehow, though, love was in the air when Roland was around.

In this case, it was a distraction for the president, causing her to overlook Oz's lack of experience and education. He felt comfortable teaching history, though. He had lived a lot of what he was teaching, and beyond that there was this wondrous and magical internet to help him out. He may not have much magic left from Oz, but he had the magic of the World Wide Web. So far he had gotten by just fine.

As for the magic from Oz, he planned to never use it. True, it faded ever so slightly if he did not use it. But he was fairly certain he would die at a natural age before it completely left him, so long as it went unused. Early on, just after leaving Oz he had used too much of it, until he got to the point where he would only use it in times of extreme need. Now, he figured he had one more use left. And he planned to never use it. It was the last souvenir he possessed of that life. He still had a few things from Oz, and from the other worlds he had visited, but the magic of Oz that coursed through his body, that was the true anchor that connected him to those joyous years.

Oz tried to look away from the screen. Henry was gone. Oz suddenly wished he had not been so noble. He wished he had tried to visit. He wished he had found the obituary sooner. It had been a couple weeks now since the death.

The hairs on the back of his neck stood. He shivered.

He heard a breathing sound. Or was it a tearing sound. No, it wasn't a sound at all. More of a feeling. The feeling of a presence. Someone, or something, was there in the room with him. Someone, or something, just outside of his perception.

He could not see them. He could not hear them. But he could feel them.

Yes, them. It was not just one.

And he felt . . . rage . . . fear . . . sadness . . . overwhelming sadness . . . despair . . .

What was this? What was happening?

And he had another feeling. Roland. A feeling about . . . Roland?

Oz stalked out of the bedroom and into the main room of his apartment. He put on his jacket and his revolvers. The jacket was from his last adventure with Roland and the Cloud Clingers, his revolvers had been with him since his time in Oz. He should have known Roland would be a part of whatever was going on. As he opened the door, he caught a glimpse of himself in the mirror. When had he gotten so old?

It took a second to realize, that wasn't him. The face staring back at him, weathered with age, mouth slack-jawed open wide, almost seemed to scream. But there was no sound. Just silence.

Wait, was that Henry? No, it was some sort of monster. Or an angel? What was he seeing?

Then the mirror exploded in a bright shower of light.

Oz stared at the creature or being or whatever it was and he felt himself turning inside out. Not physically. He felt as if his soul was slowly peeling open is flesh, being sucked into the portal.

He tried to pull away. The fear he felt was not his . . . it belonged to the creature. But the panic he felt? That was one hundred precent Oz's. His mind raced, but the only clever plan he could think of was to find Roland.

He felt relief from the creature. Yes. Get Roland. The creature released Oz. He fell to the ground as his soul reunited with his body . . . or as whatever it was this thing had done to him came undone.

* * *

Roland sat in the special chair that President Charity Underwood had made for him and placed at her dining room table. Between the two of them two candles cast a soft glow on a perfectly laid table. The gentle aroma of a perfectly cooked roast wafted into the air.

Oz almost felt bad about interrupting.

Almost.

"Who let you in?" President Underwood said, more than a little perturbed.

Oz ignored her. "Roland," Oz said, "it's an emergency. Someone from back home."

Roland glared at Oz. "My home or yours?" he hissed.

"Yes," Oz replied firmly. "Now come on."

Roland forced his scowl into a smile and nodded to President Underwood, who looked more beautiful than Oz ever remembered her looking. She did something with her hair, he thought. Maybe let it down. And make up. She never used make up. And that dress. It looked like something someone who wanted to look beautiful might wear. Not at all like the drab brown or grey or blue pant suits she usually wore.

Oz still did not care what he had interrupted. He had bigger problems, and Roland was at the center of it. He just knew it.

"Apologies," Roland said, hopping down from the chair. "Expect my return soon." His scowl returned as he marched toward Oz. "An emergency," he said. "From home," he said.

He and Oz left President Underwood's house.

Outside, Roland stopped trying to control his temper. "What could have such import that you interrupt our meal?"

Oz, not looking down, just kept walking to his car. "Just come. Somehow, I know this is your fault!"

"My fault?" Roland protested. "I did nothing!"

"I don't know what is happening, but you are at the center of it," Oz declared, "and I just know it's going to get President Underwood angry! Now get in the car!"

"President Underwood, angry because of me? The meal's interruption came from you! I ought to go right back to her!" But Roland got in the car and buckled into the child's safety seat behind Oz.

He did not speak again until they almost reached the apartment, and Oz did not mind. But finally, Roland said, "Charity, she wants to get married."

"What?"

"You heard," Roland answered. "She wants to ask me to marry her."

"And you? What do you want?"

Roland shrugged. "Love."

"Does she love you?"

Roland shrugged. "Do any love me? I would like to think, but fear the love comes from my animal magnetism or some such."

Oz nodded. "I can see the problem."

"Truth told," Roland said, "I have no love for her. I have no love for anyone in your world. The womans here do not call to my heart."

"Yeah? Why is that?"

"My heart," Roland answered, "it belongs to someone."

"Who?"

Roland shrugged yet again. "I wish I knew."

* * *

The being was well shaped, beautiful and dark.

It hung through a hole in the wall of Oz's living room. A shimmering blue hole. A portal, but a portal unlike anything Oz had ever seen. It opened into nothing.

But the being did not seem to be from that other world. Instead, the being seemed to be from in between.

"I think I know what this is," Oz said. "It's a veil walker. Creatures that live inside the veil between worlds."

Roland was transfixed. Looking at the creature with fascination. Not listening to Oz.

"I've heard of them, but only theoretically," Oz went on. "In talking with some of my traveling companions, it has come up. Ghosts and other paranormal events, they are supposedly sometimes veil walkers -- not always the souls of people with unfinished business but rather denizens of the veil that have come too close to the surface and . . . are you even hearing a word I've said?"

Roland still paid Oz no heed. Instead, he said, "They need help."

"They?"

Roland nodded. "Me, I do not know how, but I feel them. Feel their pain. Feel their fear. Feel their need."

"And what do they need?"

Tears welled in Roland's eyes. "Me."

A tendril of energy lashed out, striking Oz on the chest and knocking him down.

"You, too, apparently," Roland said.

Oz picked himself up. "And you're somehow sensing this?"

Roland looked at Oz, his face contorted into a mask of anguish. "Yes. The fabric, their home grows weak. Something tears the fabric like never before. This spot, they chose it to speak with me. This one, she remembers me. This one, she finds me. This one, she brings the others to me. You and I, we passed them when we came here."

"Let me guess," Oz sighed. "This one, she loves you?" Roland turned back to the creature. "They need protection. Too much strain on fabric tears it. Torn fabric can kill them. You and I, we have what they need."

Not wanting the answer, Oz asked, "What do I have that they need?"

"Magic," Roland said.

And Oz's heart sank.

* * *

Oz and Roland could see more of the veil walkers, but only one, the 'woman' who remembered Roland, came through the actual tear. The others were apparitions, forms seen when you weren't looking directly at them. Other people in the building were seeing them as well, judging from the screams coming from the other apartments and the sounds of running and and slamming doors.

Oz and Roland just stood in his living room in silence. Looking. Thinking. And for Oz, anyway, panicking.

Finally, Oz said, "I don't have much magic left."

"They know."

"I may not be able to patch the hole."

"A patch they do not want," Roland said. "A pocket."

Oz smiled, understanding. "That's why they are all here. Repairing this tear only helps if this is the only tear. They want a safe refuge, right? A pocket that seals them all up, together, in one safe place. All the veil walkers, in their own little pocket. It's good. It makes sense."

"Not all," Roland corrected. "Just as many as they gathered while looking for us."

"It can only be done," Oz said, "if I go in with them. Seal the pocket from inside."

Roland nodded. "Seal the pocket from within."

A loud crashing noise. Glass rained outside the sliding door on the balcony and a person followed.

"This is bad," Oz said. "Do they know they are causing problems here?"

Roland nodded again. "When you heal the tear and seal the pocket, it will stop."

Oz stepped toward the portal. "These means the last of my magic . . . and the loss of my home."

Roland jogged in front of Oz. "No. Me, I go in. You, you use your magic. Me, I act as conduit. You stay here, I stay there."

"I don't know if that will work," Oz said.

"It uses the same concept as the Cavorite and the photonic beam. The energy from one feeds the energy from the other. Instead of opening, though, it closes."

"Are you sure?"

Roland turned to the portal. "There, finally, the love I seek."

"Her?"

Oz had never seen a smile so big on Roland's tiny face. "Her."

"If you go in there, it is forever. Are you sure?"

"I felt only loss since we came here. I thought I felt loss because this world belonged to you, not to me. I thought I felt loss because my world died. But no," Roland reached out his hands and touched the thing that hung through the hole in the wall. "I felt loss because my soul touched her soul while passing through the veil. She felt the same. So when they needed help, she sought me."

"Roland, if you disappear, I'm going to lose my job."

Roland thought for a moment. "Bring me your phone."

Oz was not privy to Roland's conversation. Roland said there were private things he wished to say. But when he finishes, he told Oz, "Charity, she believes I go to an Australian outback walk-about to find myself. I asked her not to tell you the details or you would seek me. She does not connect you with my leaving. You keep your job."

"But not my magic," Oz sighed. "And not my friend."

Roland looked up at the portal. "Oz, I need your help."

Oz lifted his friend up. "Are you sure you want to go?"

"You stay, keep your life," Roland said. "I go, and keep my love."

"I'll blast you with my magic," Oz said. "The energy comes from me, but you focus it. You will shape it, pulling the veil around you and the veil walkers into a pocket."

"Just do it!"

Oz put Roland through the portal. Roland floated away from Oz into the dark nothing. The being pulled itself back through, engulfing Roland as she did.

"Now!" Roland shouted. It was the last word Oz heard from his friend.

Oz raised his hands, and focused his magic into a single stream, blasting Roland in the chest. Roland flexed his arms, bring them together as if he were pulling curtains closed.

And slowly, following his motion, the rift closed.

And then, it was gone.

And Oz was alone.

Epilogue
In Which a Bug Comes Around, a Portal Is Found, and a Frown Turns Upside-down

It was a woggle-bug. Oz was sure of it.

Oz had been walking across campus, distracted as he usually was, trying to not think about Roland and Oz and all the things that he had left behind and all the things that had left him behind and, as usual, failing utterly.

That was the reason, though, he thought he had imagined it. Thoughts of Oz had taken most of his attention lately. Thoughts of the land he once ruled. Thoughts of the power he once coveted and that, when he finally had that magical power, he came to respect and treasure. Thoughts of the magic that he had carried around for so long, using so sparingly, but had given up. He regretted none of it. How could he? Looking at his life, he had lost people, fought people, and left people behind . . . but in doing so, he had also met people, helped people, and loved people. He had become part of a makeshift family with all the earthlings who came to Oz, he had made friends with companions like Roland who shared his adventures, and he had had lovers like . . .

But he tried not to think of her. Better to think of Oz.

He still would not break the vow had had made to himself about contacting his friends. He kept his eye on them, especially Dorothy, but he refused to disrupt their lives. It took everything he had not to reach out to Em after Henry died, but he knew that the last thing she needed was a reminder of her life in the land of Oz, and any comfort he could offer her would be outweighed by the disruption he would bring.

And so, the day's classes over, he was walking across the college lawn, lost in wistful, melancholy thoughts when he saw it.

It leapt across his field of vision, appearing from seemingly nowhere and disappearing behind a tree. It was a woggle-bug of some size, far larger than the wild woggle-bugs of Oz that usually only got to be the size of a pea. It was probably one of the domesticated woggle-bugs that young Winkies liked to keep as pets.

But where had it come from? Could it possibly have come through a portal? Here? If it did, that couldn't be a coincidence. He'd been hearing rumblings from his network of "otherworld underground" contacts that portals had been becoming more commonplace. Something had happened recently, probably the same something that had caused the trouble with the Veil Walkers, something that was allowing or causing rifts to open more freely.

Oz darted around the tree to see if the bug was there. Of course, it was not. They moved too fast and erratically. If it had jumped behind the tree, surely it would have bounded off again. But where?

Out of the corner of his eye he saw the unnaturally bright colors of the woggle-bug bursting upward into the air, across the common area. The few students who milled around were too engrossed in their phones or each other to notice a peculiarly colored, abnormally sized, unusually speedy bug.

He ran across the college lawn as fast as his old legs would take him, following the small creature. Unfortunately, while they were too engrossed in their devices and relationships to notice the bug, they were not too engrossed to notice Oz himself. A few students snickered at Professor Oz, an entangled couple disengaged from their public display of affection long enough to watch him and whisper to each other, one student recorded Oz on his phone and gave the recording a snarky narration, and the last student Oz passed shouted at Oz, saying, "Yeah, sir! You're pretty fast for an old dude!"

Oz ignored it all except the compliment. He was pretty fast for an old dude. "Clean living in an alternate dimension," Oz shouted back.

The bug was not easy to follow, and but there was something that drew Oz to it. He wasn't quite able to predict where it was going, but he always seemed to be able to catch a glimpse of it when it would change direction just before it hopped out of sight.

As he followed it, slowly a feeling of anticipation rose in his chest. A feeling of longing for that lost land that shared his name. As he followed the woggle-bug, he could feel himself getting closer not just to the creature . . . but to Oz.

But even as that longing and that anticipation grew, so did a sense of dread. Was the veil between the worlds so thin, so frail, that it just Oz's longing for his old home was enough to tear it?

As much as he now yearned to be away from this mundane life of academia and as much as he desired to go through the portal and be back in Oz, he feared what this meant.

First the veil walkers. Then the whispers and rumors. And now the woggle-bug. He found himself hoping that he imagined it.

Even as he saw a streak of color disappear behind the corner of the cafeteria, he wished he imagined it.

Even as he rounded the corner himself, he prayed he imagined it.

But then, there it was. Not the woggle-bug. There, under a bush behind the cafeteria, a small portal. Just big enough for something like a woggle-bug.

The creature was nowhere to be seen. The portal was proof that he had not imagined it. He crouched down on his hands and knees and peeked through the portal. There it was. Oz.

He put his face to the portal, sticking his nose through. Smelling the Oz air.

He never thought he'd smell that again.

Oz backed up from the portal, frowning grimly. The old feelings and memories and emotions and connections and maybe even a wisp of magic washed over him. But there was no joy. This portal should not be there. This portal should not exist. Should not be stable. Nothing more than Oz's memories of Oz had created it. If, perhaps, it had led to another world Oz might have accepted the possibility of this just being a random portal, which was concerning in its own way. But this was a specific door to a world Oz was connected to. Something caused this. Something great and powerful.

And Oz hadn't been great and powerful in a long, long time.

Suddenly, from the edge of his sight, the woggle-bug made a dash for the portal. Oz stepped back. He couldn't go back, not through a portal this small, as much as he wanted to. But even if he could, there was something he needed to do on this side. And, perhaps, he was the only one on this side who could.

Oz watched it. If he could not go home, at least it could. It arced through the air, coming down toward the portal.

But just before the woggle-bug got to the portal, it closed.

It looked around, confused. Oz silently stepped behind the creature and then, with both hands, carefully picked it up. "Looks like we're both stuck here," Oz said. "Don't worry, you'll come to like it."

The woggle-bug did not answer.

"But this is proof that the fabric is weakening," Oz said. "What say you and I find out what's going on? I can't do this alone."

Oz thought for a moment. That was truth. He could not do it alone.

He smiled. The idea of breaking a vow normally sickened him. But not this time. This was a vow he would gladly break, although it took the threat of the world's destruction -- no, the threat of many worlds' destruction -- to get him to break it.

"And I have a feeling that I just may need help from some old friends . . ."

COVER GALLERY

ARTISTS ACROSS THE COMIC INDUSTRY
COVER THE OZ/WONDERLAND CHRONICLES: PRELUDE.

ARTHUR SUYDAM

BRIANNA GARCIA

ARTHUR SUYDAM'S PROPOSED COVER ART

ARTHUR SUYDAM'S REVISED
COVER ART STILL FEATURES
A BLOND SARAH AND NO
WONDERLAND CHARACTERS

BRIANNA GARCIA'S ORIGINAL
BACKGROUND DESIGN

Sketch Book
& Character Designs
By Casey Heying
& Other Fine Illustrators

SARAH

Sarah -- Sarah's life has been one harsh reality after another, and she escaped the reality of this world by entering other worlds, through the pages of books written by her favorite author: Mae Mannering. But now, with Mr. Raven at her side and helping her unlock the doors to other worlds such as Oz and Wonderland, she may finally find a true world she can escape to and call her own.

MR. RAVEN

Mr. Raven -- A denizen of the seven dimensions, little is known about what Mr. Raven is, what he wants, or why he does what he does. What he does is push and lead and encourage and discourage. Whatever his motivation, the people he manipulates (helps?) find themselves on great journeys of discovery . . . for good, or for ill.

FROGMAN

FROGMAN -- THE FROGMAN OF OZ IS A SNAPPY, FASHIONABLE CHAP. ONCE A NORMAL FROG (IF ANYTHING CAN BE CALLED NORMAL IN OZ), HE ACCIDENTALLY ATE SOME MAGICAL FOOD AND GREW TO BE HUMAN SIZE AND HAVE HUMAN SIZE INTELLIGENCE. . . AND VANITY.

GLINDA

GLINDA -- THE GREATEST PROTECTOR THE LAND OF OZ HAS EVER KNOWN, GLINDA IS A WITCH OF GREAT POWER AND PURE HEART. EVERYTHING SHE DOES IS DONE TO PROTECT THE LAND AND PEOPLE OF OZ. AND SHE WOULD GIVE UP EVERYTHING SHE HAS TO PROTECT OZ.

WICKED WITCH

THE (NEW?) WICKED WITCH -- NOT SO LONG AGO, THE LAND OF OZ WAS TORMENTED BY TWO EVIL WITCHES, THE WICKED WITCH OF THE EAST, WHO WAS DESTROYED WHEN DOROTHY'S HOUSE FELL ON HER, AND THE WICKED WITCH OF THE WEST, WHO WAS MELTED WHEN DOROTHY THREW WATER ON HER. THEY WERE SISTERS, THE ONLY TWO SISTERS IN THEIR FAMILY AND THE LAST OF THEIR FAMILY'S EVIL TRADITION OF DARK ARTS. SO WHO IS THE NEW WITCH? AND WHY DOES SHE LOOK SO MUCH LIKE THE WICKED WITCH OF THE WEST?

DOORMAN

Doorman -- The frog doorman has been doorman to the Queen of Hearts' home for years, now. As part of the serving class in the realm of Wonderland ruled over by that Queen, he has done his job diligently day in and day out.

MATRIARCH

Matriarch frog woman -- The frog people of Wonderland are hard working members of the "underclass." They are the ones who keep castles and manors running while foolish kings and mad queens rule. Of course, given the choice between working for an insane duchess and a happy, generous boss . . . well, they're loyal, but not stupid.

ALICE

ALICE -- WHEN SHE FELL DOWN THE RABBIT HOLE AS A CHILD, SHE ENTERED WONDERLAND, RETURNING AGAIN WHEN SHE STEPPED THROUGH A MIRROR, AND HER LIFE WAS CHANGED FOREVER . . . EVEN IF SHE HAS FORGOTTEN THOSE EXPERIENCES COMPLETELY. WHEN SOMEONE LEAVES ONE OF THOSE OTHER WORLDS TO RETURN HOME, THE WORLD THEY LEFT BEHIND NEVER ENTIRELY LEAVES THEM. NOW, IN ALICE'S DREAMS, SHE RETURNS TO HER MEMORIES OF WONDERLAND. WILL IT BE LONG BEFORE SHE RETURNS IN BODY, TOO?

DOROTHY

DOROTHY -- SHE WAS NOT THE FIRST FROM OUR WORLD TO VISIT OZ, BUT SHE POSSIBLY HAD MORE IMPACT ON THAT LAND THAN ANYONE ELSE, PERHAPS MORE THAN EVEN THE WIZARD HIMSELF. HER EARLY ADVENTURES WERE WELL CHRONICLED, BUT HER RETURN HOME WAS NOT VERY EVENTFUL, THAT IS, UNTIL THE DEATH OF HER UNCLE HENRY. A DEATH THAT NEVER WOULD HAVE HAPPENED HAD THEY STAYED IN OZ. OF COURSE, ALL OF THAT IS LOST TO HER MEMORY, LESS THAN A DREAM, BUT TRACES OF OZ STILL CLING TO HER.

OZ

OZ -- HE'S BEEN CALLED "GREAT." HE'S BEEN CALLED "POWERFUL." HE'S BEEN CALLED A "HUMBUG." HE'S ALL OF THAT AND MORE. OR HE HAS BEEN, IN THE PAST. MANY OF HIS ADVENTURES CAME ABOUT BECAUSE OF ACCIDENTAL CIRCUMSTANCES, LIKE A BALLOON BLOWN OFF COURSE THROUGH AN INTER-DIMENSIONAL PORTAL, AND WHILE HE MAY NOT INTEND TO BE A HERO, HE HAS LEARNED TO RISE TO THE OCCASION. A LONER, HE ALWAYS ENDS UP MAKING CONNECTIONS HE DOES NOT WANT, BUT WHEN THOSE CONNECTIONS ARE BROKEN HE DOES NOT WANT TO LOSE THEM. NO OTHER HUMAN HAS TRAVELED TO AS MANY WORLDS AS HE HAS. BUT WHEREVER HE GOES HIS HEART BELONGS TO OZ . . . AND TO THE PEOPLE HE HAS LEFT BEHIND.

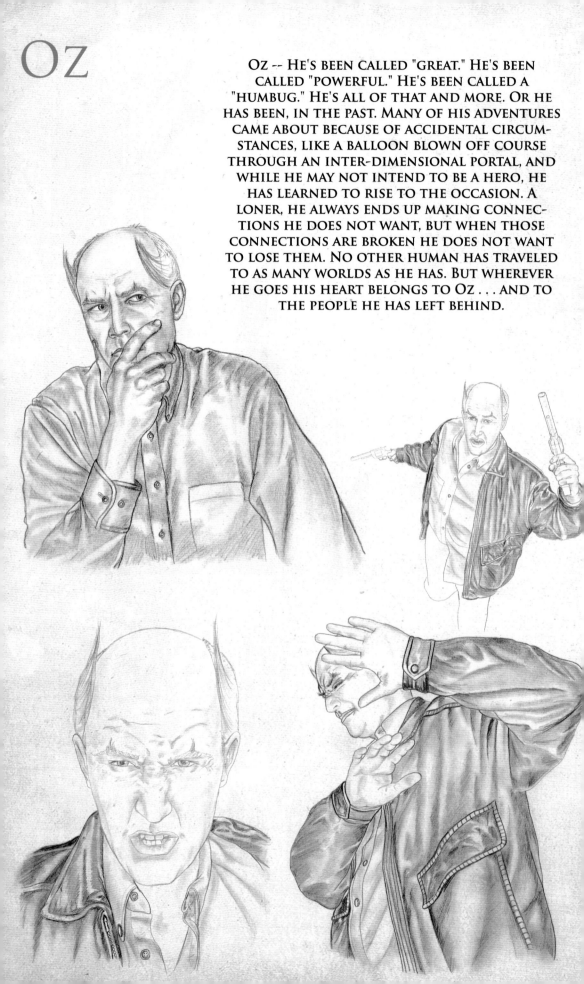

Pedro Maia's Character Sketches

Teddy Riawan's Unused Character Redesigns

And Now an Oz/Wonderland Rarity-
This All Ages Issue was meant to stand on it's own,
and be an easy way for young readers to enjoy
the Oz/Wonderland concept.

Oz/Wonderland
KIDS™

DOROTHY!?

OH DOROTHY, MY FINE CHINA!

IT'S OK AUNT EM. ALICE IS SPECIAL GUEST, AND YOU SAID THE CHINA IS FOR SPECIAL GUEST.

WELL, YES I DID... JUST BE CAREFUL, OK DEAR.

DON'T WORRY, MRS. GALE WE'LL BE EXTRA CAREFUL.

MY WORD! I THOUGHT SHE'D NEVER LEAVE!

...NOW IF ONLY WE COULD FIND THE DORMOUSE...

EEEEKKK!

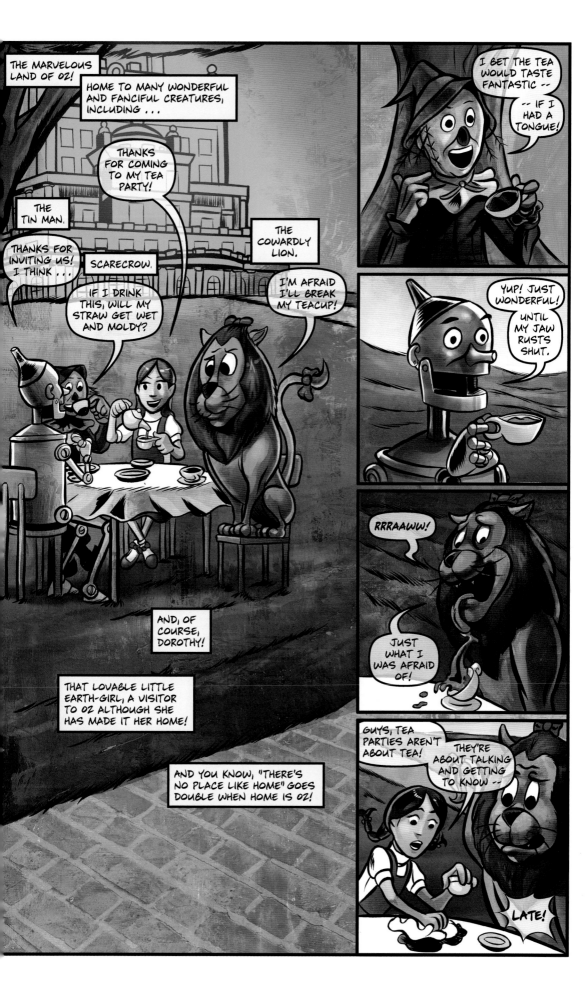

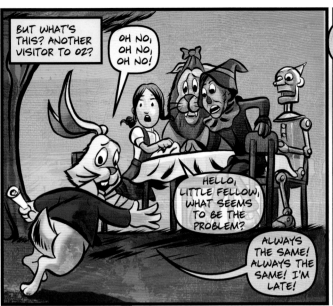

BUT WHAT'S THIS? ANOTHER VISITOR TO OZ?

OH NO, OH NO, OH NO!

HELLO, LITTLE FELLOW, WHAT SEEMS TO BE THE PROBLEM?

ALWAYS THE SAME! ALWAYS THE SAME! I'M LATE!

I HAVE TO GET A MESSAGE TO THE QUEEN BEFORE 6:00!

I JUST STOPPED TO CHECK MY HAIR IN A MIRROR -- HARES MUST LOOK GOOD WHEN PRESENTING TO A QUEEN, YOU KNOW -- AND THOSE TWEEDLES BUMPED ME THROUGH!

THEN I WAS CHASED BY THAT BEAST ...

WAS IT A KALIDAH? HUGE MONSTER WITH A TIGER HEAD AND A BEAR BODY?

I DON'T THINK IT HAD A TIGER HEAD, BUT THE BODY WAS BARE!

ALL I KNOW IS THE BEAST MAKES ME LATE! THE QUEEN WILL BE UPSET, AND AN UPSET QUEEN MEANS A CHOPPED OFF HEAD!

I'M JUST ABOUT THE SMARTEST ONE HERE, BUT I'M CONFUSED.

YOU TOO? YOU DON'T KNOW HOW GOOD IT MAKES ME FEEL TO HEAR YOU SAY THAT.

RUFF! RUFF!

OH, THE HORROR!

THE BEAST! IT APPROACHES!

WHAT KIND OF MAGIC IS THAT?

I BET THE WICKED WITCH OF THE WEST IS BEHIND THIS!

NOW I HAVE TWO RESCUES TO MAKE!

RESCUE THAT POOR LITTLE RABBIT FROM TOTO . . .

AND RESCUE TOTO FROM THE WITCH'S MIRROR TRAP!

DOROTHY, FOOLISH GIRL, THAT MIRROR IS NOT OF MY DESIGN!

I'VE NEVER SEEN IT BEFORE!

BUT WITH DOROTHY INSIDE IT, I JUST MAY HAVE FOUND A WAY TO RID OZ OF THAT MEDDLING LITTLE GIRL . . .

FOREVER!!!

MILADY, I WAS ASKED TO BRING YOU THIS MESSAGE BEFORE 6:00 . . .

FOOL! CAN'T YOU TELL I'M ABOUT TO EMBARK ON A PLAN TO RID OZ OF DOROTHY!

GIVE IT TO ME LATER!

TWO MESSAGES TO BE DELIVERED BY 6:00? COINCIDENCE? OR SOMETHING FAR MORE SINISTER?

YES, WE THINK SO TOO!

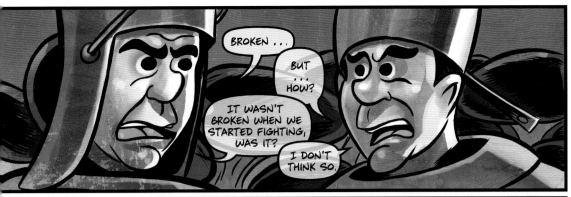

MEANWHILE, THE WICKED WITCH IS DOING WHAT SHE DOES BEST: BEING UP TO NO GOOD!

EVER SINCE SHE TOOK MY SISTER'S SHOES --

-- I'VE WANTED TO GET RID OF DOROTHY!

NOW, IF I BREAK THIS MIRROR, MAYBE SHE'LL BE STUCK ON THE OTHER SIDE AND I'LL FINALLY BE RID OF HER --

-- FOREV--

-- EEERRRRRR?

I PROBABLY SHOULD HAVE THOUGHT THAT THROUGH A BIT MORE.

OO! OO! OOO!!!

OOO! OOO!

MEANWHILE, IN OZ, AT THE LESS EXCITING TEA PARTY.

YOU KNOW, THIS TEA PARTY ISN'T BAD NOW THAT WE DON'T HAVE TO DRINK TEA.

NEXT TIME, LET'S INVITE DOROTHY TO A "TEA PARTY WITHOUT ANY TEA"!

SO, IN OTHER WORDS, A "PARTY"?

YES! RIGHT! EXACTLY!

BUT A REALLY BORING PARTY WHERE YOU DON'T DO ANYTHING!

I'M IN! YOU?

BACK IN WONDERLAND.

HMM

SO, DOES YOUR DOG DO THIS KIND OF THING OFTEN?

YES, SOMETIMES I WISH I HAD A CAT LIKE YOURS!

HEH HEH

HERE'S THE DIFFERENCE BETWEEN CATS AND DOGS:

DOGS HAVE OWNERS, CATS ARE OWNERS!

DOGS LOVE YOU. BRING YOU SLIPPERS THAT SORT OF THING CATS JUST DON'T –

--CARE.

SORRY! MAYBE I SHOULD HAVE WARNED YOU!

YEAH. MAYBE.

AT LEAST HE APOLOGIZED.

CRASH

RUFF !!!

I NEVER WOULD HAVE THOUGHT OF THAT!

SO, DOES YOUR CAT DO THIS KIND OF THING OFTEN?

YES, BUT USUALLY WHEN HE TURNS INTO A SMILE IT'S TO MAKE ME LOOK SILLY.

I ONCE MADE A LAW ABOUT SMILING AT THE QUEEN!

WHY DO YOU KEEP SAYING I'M SMILING!?!

AND THE PUNISHMENT IS --

PFFFFF FFFTTT

HOW DARE YOU!

TTTTF FFPPP!!!

HEY! THAT'S NOT MY TONGUE!

YOU DIDN'T TELL HIM TO DO THAT, DID YOU?

NO! THAT'S EVEN BETTER THAN I IMAGINED!

WHAT DID YOU JUST --

NOW YOUR WATCH WILL STAY ON 5:59! IT WILL NEVER SAY 6:00, SO YOU CAN'T BE LATE!

THAT IS HOW THINGS WORK AROUND HERE, RIGHT?

I'D SAY YOU'RE GETTING THE HANG OF THINGS, YEAH.

YOUR MAJESTY! A MISSIVE!

NOW, WHO'S THIS FROM? WHAT'S THIS ABOUT A MIRROR?

IT SAYS HERE TO DELIVER THIS MESSAGE BEFORE 6:00!

SEE! 5:59!

INDEED! GOOD JOB, RABBIT!

I THINK I NEED TO GET HOME.

MY FRIENDS WILL BE MISSING ME.

YEAH, I GUESS WE SHOULD GET YOU BACK TO THAT MIRROR.

AND SO, OUR TALE COMES TO A CLOSE . . .

I'VE BEEN DOWN THAT PART OF THE YELLOW BRICK ROAD A THOUSAND TIMES, AND I NEVER NOTICED A MIRROR BEFORE.

SAME HERE! I'VE NEVER SEEN THIS LOOKING GLASS.

I WONDER WHERE IT CAME FROM.